KT-561-007

Hannah
the Happy Ever After Fairy

by Daisy Meadows

illustrated by Georgie Ripper

ORCHARD BOOKS

www.rainbowmagic.co.uk

The Till

Welcome to Tippington Bookshop

Magic
Quill
Pen

Jack Frost's
Desk

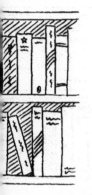

Guide to Goblins
A WINTER'S TALE ⊙
What they Never Told You
Grace the Glitter Fairy
Amber the Orange Fairy
A Sudden Chill
Finding Fairies ☆
Fairies: Do they really exist?

Summer the Holiday Fairy
Stella the Star Fairy

Fairytale Shelf

Goldilocks ⊙
Hansel and Gretel
The Princess and the Pea
The Little Matchstick Girl
The Little Mermaid
Jack and the Beanstalk
SNOW WHITE
Lady & the Tramp
Sleeping Beauty
Rapunzel
The Three Little Pigs
Beauty and the Beast
Cinderella
Puff, The Magic Dragon
Ali Baba
Red Riding Hood
The Princess + the Pauper

Children's Corner

Contents

Unhappy Endings

"Once upon a time," Kirsty Tate began, "there was a girl called Cinderella…"

Kirsty's best friend, Rachel Walker, smiled as she looked at the children in the audience. They were listening quietly to Kirsty, their eyes wide. Rachel and Kirsty had offered to read a story in the children's corner at Tippington

Bookshop, and now they were sitting
with the children in the cosy reading
area, surrounded by shelves of books.

Kirsty went on with the story. "'Oh!' Cinderella sighed. 'I'd love to go to the ball!' But her stepsisters glared at her and said…" Kirsty glanced at Rachel who was doing the voices of the nasty stepsisters.

"'You won't be going to the ball!'" Rachel said in a mean and snooty voice, making the listening children giggle. "'You're just a kitchen maid dressed in rags!'"

"Brilliant!" Kirsty whispered to Rachel, turning the page.

11

"And Cinderella's evil stepsisters made sure Cinderella did not go to the ball," Kirsty read. "Instead, she stayed at home and cleaned the house, while her stepsisters had a wonderful time. They came home and told Cinderella all about the handsome prince..."

The children gasped in horror and Kirsty's voice tailed off as she realised what she was reading. Never before had she read a story of *Cinderella* where she didn't go to the ball!

Flustered, she glanced at Rachel. Her friend was looking just as puzzled.

"Kirsty," a little girl called out, anxiously, "how will Cinderella live happily ever after if she doesn't go to the ball?"

"Check the rest of the story, Kirsty," Rachel whispered.

Kirsty flipped ahead a few pages. Cinderella was still sweeping and dusting and her stepsisters were being mean to her. Even on the very last page, Cinderella was dressed in rags and her stepsisters were complaining that she hadn't washed their clothes properly!

"It's a different story," Kirsty whispered to Rachel. "There's no happy ending!"

Some of the children were looking worried.

"Let's make it up," Rachel suggested quietly to Kirsty. "After all, we know what should happen!"

"Good idea," Kirsty agreed. She raised her voice. "So, on the night of the ball, Cinderella was sitting sadly by the fire. Suddenly, out of nowhere, there was a dazzling puff of glittering smoke!"

"It's Cinderella's Fairy Godmother!" the children shouted happily.

To Rachel and Kirsty's relief, the
children didn't realise that the girls
were making the story up as they
went along.

"…and Cinderella and the prince lived
happily ever after," Kirsty finished. The
children clapped and then started to
leave with their parents.

"Thanks for reading to us," they called
back. "We're off for a treasure hunt
now!"

"That book was really strange,
Rachel," Kirsty said, as they waved the
children off.

"I know," Rachel agreed, taking the
book and flipping through the pages.
"Do you think Charlie knows?"

The girls glanced over at Charlie,
the bookshop owner.

He was busy at the computer, but he looked up and waved at them.

"Well done, girls!" he called. "I'll be closing up soon, but you can wait here until Rachel's mum comes to collect you."

"Look, Rachel," Kirsty said, pointing at one of the bookshelves, "there are lots of fairytales here. Let's check the endings."

Rachel picked up a different copy of *Cinderella* and checked the last page.

Again the story finished with Cinderella in rags. Meanwhile, Kirsty opened *Rapunzel*.

"Rachel!" she gasped. "Rapunzel's still stuck in the tower at the end of this story!"

Rachel was already looking at *Snow White*. She showed the last page to Kirsty. "…and Snow White was trapped in her glass case forever!" Rachel read.

"All the stories have unhappy endings!" Kirsty exclaimed, flipping open *The Little Mermaid*. "Oh, no they haven't!" she corrected herself, handing the book to Rachel. "Look, the Little Mermaid does marry her prince!"

But as the girls stared at the book, the words seemed to blur and swim – the last sentence was changing before their very eyes! Now it said, "The Little Mermaid didn't marry the prince, and she didn't live happily ever after."

"This is very weird!" Kirsty gasped, reaching for a pop-up *Sleeping Beauty.*
"It seems like magic!"

"Yes, but it can't be fairy magic," Rachel added. "Not with sad endings!"

The girls knew all about fairy magic. They were friends with the fairies, and had

helped them many times before when cold, icy Jack Frost and his goblin servants were causing trouble.

Kirsty opened Sleeping Beauty and a beautiful silver and blue cardboard castle popped up. The next moment, a glittering shower of silver fairy dust burst from the book and swirled around the girls. As the sparkles drifted down, Rachel and Kirsty saw a tiny fairy perched on the castle balcony!

"Hello, girls!" she called eagerly, waving at them.

A Sneaky Thief

The fairy flew up to join Rachel
and Kirsty, her blue dress floating around
her. She wore a daisy-chain necklace
and belt, and dainty blue ballet shoes.

"I'm Hannah the Happy
Ever After Fairy," she said, as
she perched on Rachel's shoulder.
"And I really need your help, girls!"

"No problem!" Kirsty said quickly.
"What's happened?"

"Is it something to do with the unhappy
endings?" Rachel asked.

Hannah nodded, her blonde ringlets
bobbing. "I'm in charge of the magical
Quill Pen in Fairyland," she explained.
"Yesterday Jack Frost sneaked into the
palace. He stole the Jewel Fairies' magical
wands, and this morning I realised he
must have taken the Quill Pen as well!"

"What does the Quill Pen do?" Kirsty asked anxiously.

"It has the power to write fairytales for the human world," said Hannah. "But not only that – the magic pen can also change them!"

"Oh!" Rachel gasped. "So that's what Jack Frost's doing with the Quill Pen. He's rewriting all the endings of the fairytales to make them miserable!"

"Yes," Hannah replied. Her wings drooped and she looked very sad.

"When Jack Frost writes an unhappy ending with the magic Quill Pen, every copy of that story in every bookshop, library, school or home around the world is changed! All he has to do is write the title of the story he wants to change at the top of the page."

The girls stared at each other in horror.

"That's terrible!" Kirsty cried. "We have to stop him!"

"Yes, we must find Jack Frost and get the magic Quill Pen back!" Rachel agreed firmly.

"But what about the Jewel Fairies?" Kirsty asked. "They need their magic wands back too."

"That's OK," smiled Hannah. "The Jewel Fairies have organised a treasure hunt to find them. Oh, I knew you'd want to help, girls!" she said gratefully. "But it's going to be very difficult. We don't know where Jack Frost is, only that he escaped into the human world with the Quill Pen!"

Just then the shop bell jingled as a customer came in.

"Charlie's just about to close, so that's probably my mum," Rachel said as Hannah hid behind her hair.

Hannah and the girls poked their heads round the bookshelves to see if Mrs Walker had arrived.

But, instead of Rachel's mum, standing
just inside the door, and staring round
the bookshop with an icy gaze, was
Jack Frost himself!

A Cool Customer

Rachel and Kirsty could hardly believe
their eyes. Jack Frost had used his magic
to make himself much taller. Icicles hung
from his beard and he looked more
frightening than ever! He carried a large
bag, and there were six ugly goblins with
him.

Hannah put her wand to her lips. "Don't make a sound, girls," she whispered. "The Quill Pen must be in that bag!"

Rachel and Kirsty watched as Jack Frost stalked over to the till.

"I'm sorry, we're just about to close—" Charlie began, but then he glanced up and saw his new customer, and his mouth fell open in amazement.

Jack Frost raised his wand. "With this magic spell of mine, I freeze you here in space and time. When I leave you will be free, but you will not remember me!" he chanted.

Rachel and Kirsty
watched in alarm
as Charlie froze
right where he
stood, the look
of amazement
still on his face.
Ice frosted
over his hair
and clothes, and

long, glittering icicles hung
from his nose.

"What's Jack Frost doing here?"
whispered Kirsty. Hannah and
Rachel shrugged, but just then Jack
Frost turned to his goblins.

"I've changed all the fairytales
I can think of," he told them.
"But there must be more."

He pointed at the bookshelves with his wand. "Find any which still have happy endings and bring them to me!"

Rachel and Kirsty looked at each other in panic. They were right in the middle of the fairytale section!

"This way, girls!" Hannah whispered, flying into the next aisle.

Rachel and Kirsty crept after her, away from the fairytales.

Once out of sight, they peeped round the bookshelves to watch Jack Frost and his goblins.

The goblins were fighting with each other, pushing and shoving and trying to be the first to find the fairytales.

"Get out of my way!" cried one. "No, I want to find a fairytale for Jack Frost!" yelled another. "They're making a terrible mess," Rachel whispered, as the goblins started pulling books off the shelves and tossing them aside. Some of the goblins were standing on each other's shoulders to reach the higher shelves and then throwing the books to the floor.

"Look at Jack Frost," said Hannah.
Jack Frost had made his way to the
shop desk where he was
now taking two piles
of paper out of his
bag. The girls
could see that
the pages in
one pile had
writing on
them, but
the pages in the
other were blank.
Once the papers
were arranged on the
desk, Jack Frost opened his bag again
and carefully drew out a long feather
that glittered with all the colours of
the rainbow.

"The magic Quill Pen!" Hannah breathed.

The Quill Pen shimmered in the shop lights as Jack Frost picked up a blank page.

"There won't be a single happy ever after left in any of the fairytales by the time I've finished!" he said, grinning nastily to himself as he began to write. Where the pen touched the paper, magical, multi-coloured sparkles shot in all directions.

"We have to get that pen back!" whispered Rachel.

"But how?" asked Kirsty with a frown.

Suddenly, a shout from one of the goblins startled the girls.

"This book's still got a happy ending!" the goblin cried, waving a copy of *Hansel and Gretel*. "I'll take it to Jack Frost!"

"No, I saw it first!" another goblin yelled, making a grab for the book. "Give it here!"

But the goblin holding the book dashed off towards Jack Frost.

The other goblin immediately gave chase, shrieking with rage. He threw himself at the first goblin and grabbed his legs, sending him crashing into

Jack Frost's table.
Both piles of
paper went
flying.

"You fools!"
roared
Jack Frost.

One of the
pages landed
near Rachel, and she
picked it up. "Cinderella doesn't go
to the ball, she doesn't marry the
prince and she lives horribly ever
after!" it said on the page in
rainbow-coloured ink.

"These scattered pages must
be all the unhappy endings Jack
Frost has written with the Quill
Pen," Hannah whispered.

"How can I get any work done with
you idiots around?" Jack Frost yelled
at the nervous goblins. He grabbed his
wand. "So you cannot bother me at
all, I hereby make you quiet and small!"
he shouted.

A cloud of icy fairy dust streamed
from Jack Frost's wand and filled the
shop. It swirled around the goblins,
who immediately shrank to fairy-size.

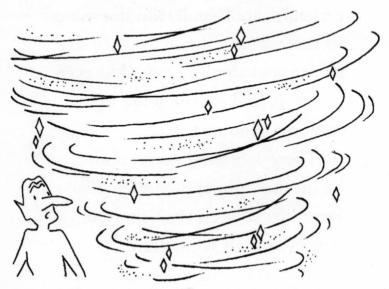

Hannah quickly zoomed up to the ceiling away from the magic dust, but Rachel and Kirsty were caught in the spell.

"Kirsty!" Rachel gasped, as the magic dust cleared. "We've shrunk too!"

Kirsty looked at Rachel. "We're the same size as Hannah now, just like when the fairies make us small," she agreed, as Hannah flew back to join them. "But, look," she went on, pointing at her friend's shoulders. "This time we haven't got any wings!"

Girls Go Into Action

"What did you say?" Rachel asked with a frown. Kirsty's voice was so tiny and quiet, she could hardly hear her friend talking! It was only when she glanced over her own shoulder that she realised what Kirsty meant.

The girls stared at each other in

dismay. They had become fairy-sized many
times before to help the fairies – but then
they'd always had wings!

On the other side of the shelves,
which now towered above the girls like
skyscrapers, Jack Frost was picking up
his papers and grumbling at the goblins.

"He's left the Quill Pen on the desk," Rachel pointed out. "Now's our chance!"

"Can you make us human-sized again?" Kirsty asked Hannah eagerly.

Hannah shook her head. "I can't undo Jack Frost's spell," she replied.

"That means that even if we get onto the desk, we can't pick up the Quill Pen," Kirsty said glumly. "It's too big."

"Well, I can't make you big, but I can make the Quill Pen small!" Hannah told her.

"Brilliant!" Kirsty sighed with relief. "But how do we get onto the desktop? It's too high for us to reach!"

"Look," Rachel said, pointing to a stack of books on the floor. "Hannah, could you magic those books into a staircase?"

Hannah nodded and the girls watched as magic sparkles flew from her wand. The books immediately organised themselves into a staircase and Rachel and Kirsty ran over and began to climb.

"Nearly there, girls!" Hannah called encouragingly, as she fluttered above them. "Keep going!"

As she climbed higher, Rachel glanced over her shoulder.
Her heart sank
when she saw
the goblins.
They were jumping
up and down and
pointing – the girls
had been spotted!

"Kirsty!" Rachel gasped. "The goblins have seen us, and they're trying to warn Jack Frost!"

Kirsty glanced at Jack Frost. "He hasn't noticed yet," she said. "He can't hear the goblins now they're so small and quiet, but we'd better hurry!"

Rachel and Kirsty stepped off the last book and onto the desk. They'd made it – and they could see the magical Quill Pen shimmering and sparkling not far away! But the goblins had given up trying to warn Jack Frost and were now climbing up the book staircase after the girls.

"They're coming!" Kirsty gasped. "Quick, Hannah, make the Quill Pen smaller!"

Hannah sent a swirl of fairy dust towards the pen, shrinking it to the size of a teaspoon.

"But the goblins are blocking your way down, girls!" she warned. "How are you going to get away?"

Rachel looked around desperately for an escape route as the goblins neared the desktop, but she couldn't see a way out. There was nothing on the desk except the Quill Pen and some blank pages, and the desk was far too high for them to jump off.

Suddenly, as she stared at the magic pen, Rachel had an idea. She knew the Quill Pen had the power to change stories, so what if she made everything happening right now into a story? A story called *Hannah the Happy Ever After Fairy*. If she wrote the ending to the story now, surely the pen's magic would make it happen!

Quickly, Rachel grabbed the sparkling Quill Pen.

"What are you doing?" asked Kirsty, puzzled.

But Rachel didn't have time to reply. On top of one of the blank pages she

wrote the title of her story: *Hannah the Happy Ever After Fairy*. But rainbow-coloured sparkles fizzed from the magic pen as she wrote, and the glitter of magic caught Jack Frost's eye.

"Who's using my Quill Pen?" he shouted from the back of the shop.

"Hurry, Rachel!" Kirsty gasped. "The goblins have reached the top of the staircase, and Jack Frost's seen us. He's raising his wand to cast a spell!"

The Wind of Change

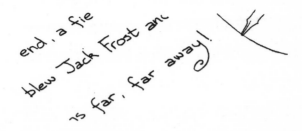

"I've almost finished!" Rachel cried.

Kirsty peered over Rachel's shoulder to see what she had written. Under the title, it said, "In the end, a fierce wind blew Jack Frost and all his goblins far, far away!"

The moment Rachel finished writing "away", Kirsty felt a strong wind begin to

pick up. Just as the goblins stepped onto
the desktop, the wind whirled them off
their feet and swept them up into
the air. The goblins shouted in confusion.

Jack Frost rushed towards the desk,
pointing his wand at the girls. But in
a flash the wind scooped him up too.

"Put me down!" Jack Frost cried as he

was lifted off his feet and carried along helplessly on the strong breeze. "I'm the great Jack Frost! Put me down, I say!"

As Hannah and the girls watched, the shop door flew open and the wind blew Jack Frost and all his goblins outside into the street. Then it carried them off high into the sky, still struggling and shouting.

"Well done, Rachel!" Hannah laughed, clapping her hands.

But Rachel was still writing. Curious, Kirsty and Hannah looked to see what else she had added.

"The fairytales got their happy endings back, and Charlie, Kirsty, Hannah and Rachel lived happily ever after!"

Immediately, Rachel and Kirsty shot back up to their normal size and had to scramble down off the desk. To their delight, they saw that Charlie wasn't frozen any more either. He was typing away at the computer, just as he had been doing when Jack Frost arrived. He gave the girls a cheerful smile, as Hannah ducked out of sight behind Kirsty.

"I expect your mum will be here soon, Rachel," he said, and disappeared into the stockroom.

"What a relief!" Hannah smiled. "Jack Frost's spell means he doesn't remember anything. Now, let's tidy up!"

She waved her wand. The girls watched as the books magically lifted themselves off the floor and jumped back onto the shelves in a swirl of glittering fairy magic.

"And if you ever need help with your own stories," Hannah went on with a smile, "just come to Fairyland and find me!"

"Thank you," laughed Rachel.

"Don't forget the Quill Pen," Kirsty said, picking up the tiny, feathery pen and handing it carefully to Hannah.

"Everyone in Fairyland will be very grateful," said Hannah, her eyes shining. "And so will everyone who reads fairytales! Let's hope the Jewel Fairies are as lucky in finding their wands. Goodbye, girls. Thank you!"

"Goodbye!" Rachel and Kirsty called.
"Say hello to the Jewel Fairies for us!"

And Hannah and the Quill Pen
disappeared in a cloud of magical sparkles.

"What are you doing?" Rachel asked, as
Kirsty hurried over to the children's corner.

"I just want to check," Kirsty replied.
She picked up the copy of Cinderella
they had been reading to the children,
and opened it at the last page.

Rachel and Kirsty beamed at each other, for the fairytale ended just as it should: "Cinderella married her prince and they lived happily ever after!"

The Rainbow Magic Treasure Hunt

Calling all Rainbow Magic fans
– the fairies need YOUR help!

Wicked Jack Frost has stolen
7 precious, glittering Jewel Fairy wands
and hidden them in 7 secret locations all over the countryside.

For your chance to WIN one of the 7 magical wands
AND to feature in a Rainbow Magic book
you must solve the clues in our Rainbow Magic Treasure Hunt!

To take part, all you have to do is:

1) Solve the special Treasure Hunt code on the opposite page.
2) Log on to **www.rainbowmagic.co.uk**, enter the special code
and select the region nearest to where you live.
3) Download your own special Rainbow Magic Treasure Map
and get your first Treasure Hunt clue telling you how to begin!

The first clue will be on the website on **Friday 3 July 2009**
and the Fun Day Fairies will be revealing a clue
every Friday for 7 weeks until **Friday 14 August 2009**,
when the last clue will be revealed.

Good Luck!

Treasure Hunt only open to UK and Republic of Ireland residents.
No purchase required. For full terms and conditions please see www.hachettechildrens.co.uk/terms

Special Treasure Hunt Code

Ruby the Red Fairy
has created this special code to start
your Treasure Hunt adventure!
Discover the magical word using the
fairy picture code below. Now log on to:
www.rainbowmagic.co.uk
and enter the special word. Select the region nearest
to where you live and get ready to join the Treasure Hunt!

A = ♥   H = ❄   O = ❀   V = ╱

B = ❀   I = ⬡   P = ⚡   W = ☁

C = 🐝   J = 🍃   Q = ◊   X = ●

D = ◆   K = 🧁   R = 🍒   Y = ❧

E = ☆   L = 🐸   S = 🦋   Z = 🎀

F = 🍄   M = ■   T = ☁

G = 🏰   N = 🎈   U = ♪

The magical code word is:

A   m   e   t   h   y   s   t

Ruby the Red Fairy
Choose Your Own Magic

Choose your own magical path through the story and rescue Ruby the Red Fairy from the clutches of wicked Jack Frost!

Available July 2009!

978-1-40830-789-2

Tesh Te

Meet the Green Fairies in September 2009!

NICOLE
THE BEACH FAIRY
978-1-40830-474-7

ISABELLA
THE AIR FAIRY
978-1-40830-475-4

EDIE
THE GARDEN FAIRY
978-1-40830-476-1

CORAL
THE REEF FAIRY
978-1-40830-477-8

LILY
THE RAINFOREST FAIRY
978-1-40830-478-5

MILLY
THE RIVER FAIRY
978-1-40830-480-8

CARRIE
THE SNOW CAP FAIRY
978-1-40830-479-2